To Mum and Dad
~ JK

To the best parents I could ever have:
thank you, Mum and Dad!
~ L B

LITTLE TIGER PRESS LTD,
an imprint of the Little Tiger Group
1 The Coda Centre,
189 Munster Road, London SW6 6AW
www.littletiger.co.uk
First published in Great Britain 2017

Text copyright © John Kelly 2017
Illustrations copyright © Laura Brenlla 2017

John Kelly and Laura Brenlla have asserted their rights to be
identified as the author and illustrator of this work under
the Copyright, Designs and Patents Act, 1988

A CIP catalogue record for this book is available from the British Library

Printed in China • LTP/1400/1808/0217

2 4 6 8 10 9 7 5 3 1

HIBERNATION HOTEL

John Kelly

Laura Brenlla

LITTLE TIGER

LONDON

It was WAY past hibernation time but Bear just COULD NOT sleep!

His cave, as usual, was far too crowded. Racoon snored. Beaver fidgeted. And Skunk, frankly, was a little bit whiffy.

"I've had enough of
being treated like
a big furry mattress,"
Bear harrumphed.

So he got up, made a phone call, and booked himself into a fancy hotel.

"Ahhh," said Bear as he drove away. "Peace and quiet at last!"

The hotel was HUGE and fancy – just like the receptionist's moustache! Bear tried not to stare at it as he checked in.

"Would Sir like a wake-up call?" asked the receptionist.

"Yes, please," said Bear. "March 1st."

The bellboy showed Bear to his room —
it was BIGGER than his whole cave!
"THIS IS THE LIFE!" whooped Bear,
bouncing up and down on the bed.

"And look at these snacks!"
Bear cheered.

He didn't know which
one to eat. So he ate
them all . . .

then washed
everything down
with a huge slurp
of water.

Bear used every bottle of shampoo ... and all the hot water too!

Then he dried his hair, brushed his teeth ...

and flopped, exhausted, into bed.
"Perfect!" he yawned as he closed
his eyes, and . . .

He stomped down the corridor.
"Would you mind keeping the noise down?"
he growled, ever so politely. "I am TRYING
to hibernate!"

His fellow guests were only too happy to oblige.
Bear stumbled back to bed.

But no matter how much he tossed and turned,
Bear just could not sleep.

"HUMPH!" he moaned. "This bed is TOO squishy
for a big-boned Bear!" So he flung the bedding
onto the floor and crawled beneath the heap.

"MMMM! Toasty!" sighed Bear snuggling down.
He grew toastier, then roastier until . . .

"BOTHERATION!" he cried. "Now I'm too blinking HOT!"
He threw off the bedding, opened the window wide
and let the cool night air ruffle his fur.
Soon Bear wasn't hot anymore, but he wasn't sleepy either.

"Maybe a spot of TV will help me snooze," he sighed,
and began to flick through the channels.
There was nothing on but wildlife shows,
and for some reason they made Bear feel sad.
So he turned the TV off and flopped back
into bed.

Bear lay in the dark, wide awake and all alone.

"I just don't get it," he huffed. "I'm in a luxurious bed, with no snoring, fidgeting, or skunky whiffs. And I STILL can't sleep!"

Deep in the pit of Bear's tummy there was a strange, hollow, empty feeling.

And right then Bear knew EXACTLY why he couldn't sleep.

"I'M HUNGRY!" he howled.
"A bear can't be expected to
sleep on an empty tummy!"
    Bear phoned room service.
"I'd like to order the menu,
please," he said. "All of it."

A few minutes later there was a knock on the door. The bellboy wheeled in the trolley. Bear licked his lips, and lifted the largest cover. But instead of a fabulous feast he found . . .

... his furry friends!
"What are YOU doing here!"
bellowed Bear.

"We missed you!" they cried.
"We can't get to sleep without you!"

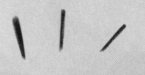

Soon Bear was buried beneath a pile of his sleepy pals.
And even though Racoon snored, Beaver fidgeted,
and Skunk was still a bit whiffy,
Bear didn't mind.

He was *finally* fast asleep.

More fantastic stories about friendship from Little Tiger Press!

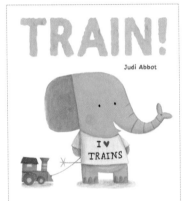

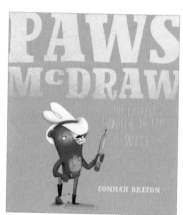

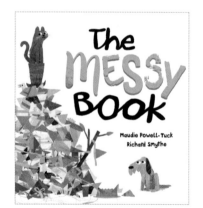

For information regarding any of the above titles
or for our catalogue, please contact us:
Little Tiger Press,
1 The Coda Centre,
189 Munster Road,
London SW6 6AW
Tel: 020 7385 6333
E-mail: contact@littletiger.co.uk
www.littletiger.co.uk